NICK®

SpongeBob SquarePants™

Phonics Reading Program

Book 9 · long a

✓ P9-DED-621

# SPONGEBOB SAVES THE DAY

by Sonia Sander

## SCHOLASTIC INC.

New York   Toronto   London   Auckland   Sydney
Mexico City   New Delhi   Hong Kong   Buenos Aires

"Hopping clams!" cried SpongeBob. "Gary is gone!"

"I must be brave and go save Gary!" said SpongeBob as he put on his cape.

SpongeBob took off
to find Gary.
He raced across the sky.
He looked high and low.

SpongeBob spotted some bad guys and followed them to a cave. "Meow," said Gary.

SpongeBob chased the bad guys. He saved Gary. SpongeBob gave the bad guys over to the cops.

"I am glad you are
safe, Gary,"
said SpongeBob.
"I'll never let anyone
take you away again."

"For capturing those criminals and making Bikini Bottom safe again, please take this key to the city," said the mayor.

SpongeBob woke from his dream. "Aw, Gary, you are always safe with me," he said.